Dear Parent:

Psst . . . you're looking at the Super Secret Weapon of Reading. It's called comics.

STEP INTO READING® COMIC READERS are a perfect step in learning to read. They provide visual cues to the meaning of words and helpfully break out short pieces of dialogue into speech balloons.

Here are some terms commonly associated with comics:
   PANEL: A section of a comic with a box drawn around it.
   CAPTION: Narration that helps set the scene.
   SPEECH BALLOON: A bubble containing dialogue.
   GUTTER: The space between panels.

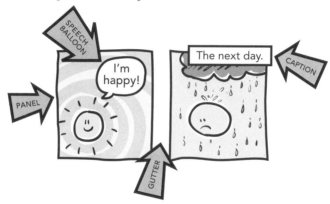

Tips for reading comics with your child:

• Have your child read the speech balloons while you read the captions.
• Ask your child: What is a character feeling? How can you tell?
• Have your child draw a comic showing what happens after the book is finished.

STEP INTO READING® COMIC READERS are designed to engage and to provide an empowering reading experience. They are also fun. The best-kept secret of comics is that they create lifelong readers. And that will make you the real hero of the story!

Jennifer L. Holm and Matthew Holm
Co-creators of the Babymouse and Squish series

Special thanks to Diane Reichenberger, Cindy Ledermann, Jocelyn Morgan, Tanya Mann, Emily Kelly, Sharon Woloszyk, Michelle Cogan, Allison Monterosso, David Wiebe, and ARC Productions.

Published in the United States by Random House Children's Books, a division of Random House, Inc., 1745 Broadway, New York, NY 10019, and in Canada by Random House of Canada Limited, Toronto.

Visit us on the Web!
StepIntoReading.com
randomhouse.com/kids

Educators and librarians, for a variety of teaching tools, visit us at RHTeachersLibrarians.com

ISBN 978-0-385-37121-6 (trade) — ISBN 978-0-375-97187-7 (lib. bdg.)

Printed in the United States of America   10 9 8 7 6 5 4 3

Random House Children's Books supports the First Amendment and celebrates the right to read.

A COMIC READER

Adapted by Kristen L. Depken

Based on the screenplay by Robin Stein

Random House New York

The Dreamhouse is so amazing!

At the Dreamhouse, Nikki and Teresa are helping Barbie pick out an outfit.

Both.

It's our forty-third anniversary!

It's the forty-third anniversary of the first time we held hands!

You can't find a greeting card for that!

So I made one.

Barbie can't wait for her date!
Her outfit is almost perfect.

My little rhinestone-studded butterfly barrette.

Barbie's closet . . .

is . . .

AMAZING!

Meanwhile . . .

I'm so ready for our date!

Barbie gives Teresa and Nikki a tour of her closet.

I've got clothes from every career I've ever had.

Is Barbie not the coolest friend ever?

She's fun, generous . . .

. . . and exactly my size!

Actually, Teresa, it's a great way for me to test new hair and makeup looks.

Ooh! Sounds like fun.

Let's try it!

They get right to work. . . .

Hours later . . .

Back in the closet . . .

Awww, I wouldn't say for nothing. Didn't we have fun?

And I found this cute necklace that will really put my outfit over the top.

They slide
down a long dark chute . . .

and land on Barbie's front steps!

Thanks for all your help, girls! You're the best friends ever!